Jim Henson's™
DOOZERS™
Catch a Ride

adapted by Cordelia Evans
based on the screenplay written by Kati Rocky

Ready-to-Read

Simon Spotlight
New York London Toronto Sydney New Delhi

SIMON SPOTLIGHT

An imprint of Simon & Schuster Children's Publishing Division

1230 Avenue of the Americas, New York, New York 10020

This Simon Spotlight edition August 2015

© 2015 The Jim Henson Company. JIM HENSON'S mark & logo, DOOZERS mark & logo, characters and elements are trademarks of The Jim Henson Company. All Rights Reserved.

All rights reserved, including the right of reproduction in whole or in part in any form.

SIMON SPOTLIGHT, READY-TO-READ, and colophon are registered trademarks of Simon & Schuster, Inc.

For information about special discounts for bulk purchases, please contact Simon & Schuster Special Sales at 1-866-506-1949 or business@simonandschuster.com.

Manufactured in the United States of America 0715 LAK

10 9 8 7 6 5 4 3 2 1

ISBN 978-1-4814-3215-3 (hc)

ISBN 978-1-4814-3214-6 (pbk)

ISBN 978-1-4814-3216-0 (eBook)

Chief Doozer has

a special mission

for the Pod Squad.

Spike, Daisy Wheel, Flex, and Molly Bolt love special missions!

"We need to figure out how big Doozer Creek is," Chief Doozer tells them.

"Put flags in the four corners.

Then we will know how far to measure."

"We should have a race!"

says Spike.

"We can each pick a corner.

Whoever plants a flag in

their corner first, wins!"

"I will go east," says Flex.

He jumps in the Podmobile.

"I will go west,"

says Daisy Wheel.

She turns on her jet pack.

"I will go south,"

says Spike.

He climbs on his Doozycle.

"Wait!" Molly Bolt says.

"How will I go north?"

"I forgot you do not have
a ride!" says Spike.

The Pod Squad decides
to build Molly Bolt
her own vehicle.

"We can build you a

Podmobile!" says Flex.

Molly Bolt tries

the Podmobile.

The seat moves up and down.

"I like how big
the Podmobile is,
but the ride is bumpy,"
she says.

"You will love

the Doozycle!"

Spike says.

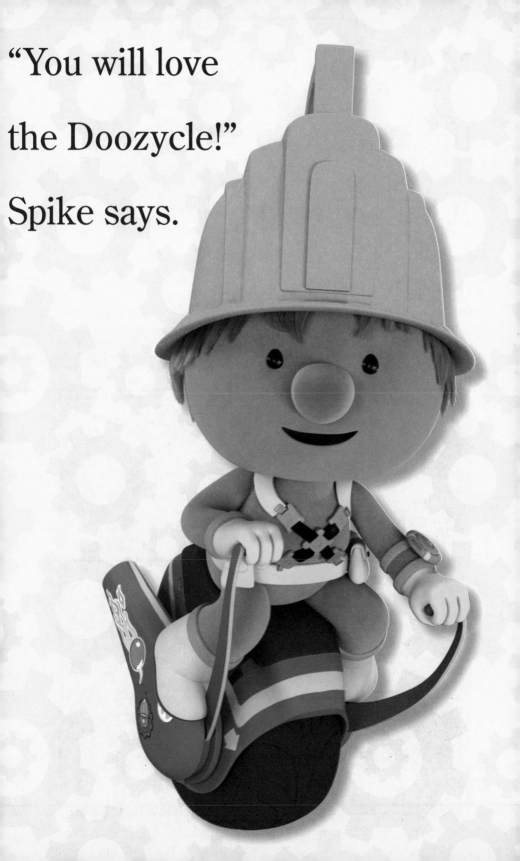

Molly Bolt tries

the Doozycle.

It is hard to stay

on the seat.

"The Doozcyle is fast,

but not comfy," she says.

"We saved the best

for last. My jet pack!"

cries Daisy Wheel.

Molly Bolt tries

the jet pack.

She flies into the air.

But she does not know

how to land!

"The jet pack is fun," she says when she is back on the ground.

"But it is hard to steer."

None of the vehicles
are right for Molly Bolt.

"Maybe Professor
Gimbal can help us!"
says Spike.

"Molly Bolt does not like
any of our rides,"
Spike tells him.

"You should ask Molly Bolt how she likes to ride," Professor Gimbal says.

Molly Bolt replies,

"I like going fast.

I like having storage.

I like a comfy seat.

And I like gliding!"

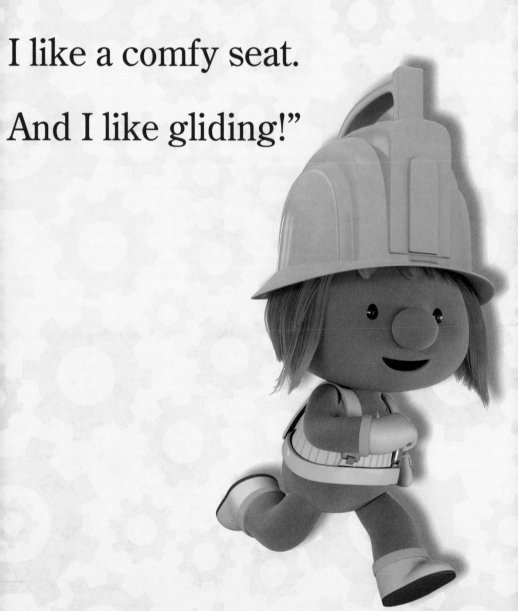

The Pod Squad designs

the perfect ride.

It has big wheels, a trunk,

and sails shaped like

butterfly wings!

"The Drive-n-Sail!"

says Molly Bolt.

They work together

to build the Drive-n-Sail.

"Now the race to plant
the flags is on!"
Molly Bolt says.
The Pod Squad takes off.

And Molly Bolt wins!

"There is nothing to it when you do, do, do it!" cheers the Pod Squad.